W9-ATJ-359

Dedicated to Patsy Rose

Patsy Rose, better known as "Ms. Patsy," is the children's librarian at Orange Beach Public Library. Our boys, along with so many other children, have benefited from the wonderful programs and events she has organized. Ms. Patsy does, indeed, make reading fun!

Henry Hodges Needs a Friend

Published in Nashville, Tennessee, by Tommy Nelson. Tommy Nelson is an imprint of Thomas Nelson. Thomas Nelson is a registered trademark of HarperCollins Christian Publishing, Inc.

Illustrated by Colleen Madden

Tommy Nelson titles may be purchased in bulk for educational, business, fund-raising, or sales promotional use. For information, please e-mail SpecialMarkets@ThomasNelson.com.

ISBN-13: 978-0-529-11576-8

Library of Congress Cataloging-in-Publication Data

Andrews, Andy, 1959-
Henry Hodges and a new friend / by Andy Andrews.
pages cm
Summary: Henry Hodges is a very lonely boy until his parents decide he needs a pet that is just as special as he is.
ISBN 978-0-529-11576-8 (jacketed hardcover) [1. Stories in rhyme. 2. Loneliness--Fiction. 3. Pet adoption--Fiction. 4. Friendship--Fiction.] I. Title.
PZ8.3.A54867Hen 2015
[E]--dc23
2014013268

Printed in China

15 16 17 18 19 20 DSC 6 5 4 3 2

Mfr: DSC / Shenzhen, China / May 2015 / PO #9348450

Henry Hodges Needs a Friend

A Division of Thomas Nelson Publishers

NASHVILLE MEXICO CITY RIO DE JANEIRO

Henry Hodges was one
Of the **loneliest** boys.
No friends lived near him;
He didn't like toys.

There was never a soul
For young Henry to meet.
His house was the last
On a long dead-end street.

Henry wandered outside
To his old tire swing,
Just to wonder what **boredom**
This new day would bring.

But his mother's eyes twinkled.
"Don't **worry**. Don't fret.
A friend's what you need,
So a friend's what you'll get!"

"Son, you are special,"
Father said with a grin.
"We'll look high and look low
For the **perfect** new friend."

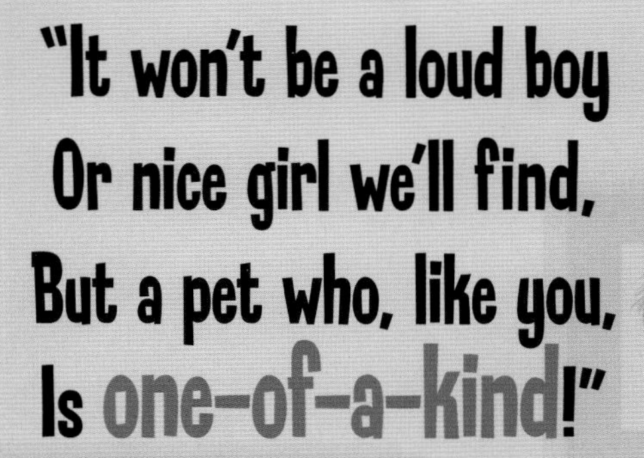

"It won't be a loud boy
Or nice girl we'll find,
But a pet who, like you,
Is one-of-a-kind!"

One-of-a-kind? Henry thought.
Hmmm—what could that be?
A kitten who barks
Or a pig who climbs trees?

Could it be a big hamster
Who flies through the air?
Or a turtle who sings
And has wild, wavy hair?

ARF, ARF, ARF!
yooouu... get meout of my shell...

Perhaps a goldfish with **antlers**?

Or a **cool** purple fox!

Hey, a goat with **ten** legs
That looks funny in socks?

Which would I choose?
Henry thought with a laugh.
A joke-telling beaver
or a short-necked giraffe?

So how much wood would a woodchuck chuck if a woodchuck could chuck wood?

A porcupine with quills
That are **softer** than silk

Or a cow for my backpack
Who gives chocolate milk?

A figure-skating hippo
Would really be nice.
But he'd eat way too much
And **break** through the ice.

Henry smiled and kept trying
To figure it out.
A one-of-a-kind friend?
Well, he had his doubts.

A shelter for animals?
That's a **great** place to look!
There he'd search for a pet,
Every cranny and nook.

And so Henry looked.
He explored every hall,
When finally his search
Ended once and for all.

There curled in a corner
Covered up in brown spots
Was the loneliest pup
Just filled with sad thoughts.

As Henry sat down,
The pup jumped in his lap.
And the boy stated proudly,
"Your new name is **Hap!**"

"It's a nickname for Happy,
And that's just what you'll be.
You'll have a friend always
Now that you're with me."

Cats can
be verrrry
sneaky

Then Henry hugged Hap,
And they rolled on the ground,
The air filled with **laughing**
And slobbery sounds.

Hap licked Henry's ears . . .
And his mouth . . . and his nose.
Hap chewed the boy's shoestrings
And nibbled his toes.

Henry now had his friend
And was lonely no more.
Once there were three Hodges,
And now there were four.

If we're lonely or sad,
God knows just what we need.
And for Henry, his Hap
Was the best choice indeed.

Henry didn't need a funny pet,
Colored yellow or blue,
But a one-of-a-kind friend,
Just like your friends need **YOU**!

More Favorite Stories from Andy Andrews

THE BESTSELLING BOOK THAT REVEALS EVERYTHING WE DO MATTERS!

Andy's timeless tale shows children that even our smallest actions can have powerful consequences. Maybe you will be the kid who changes the world!

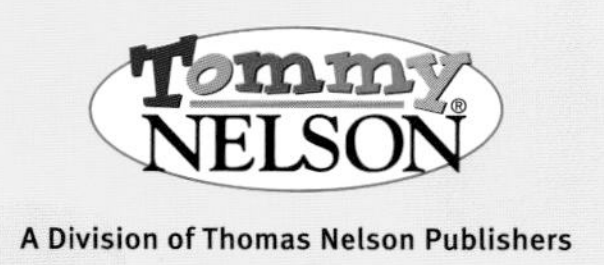

A Division of Thomas Nelson Publishers

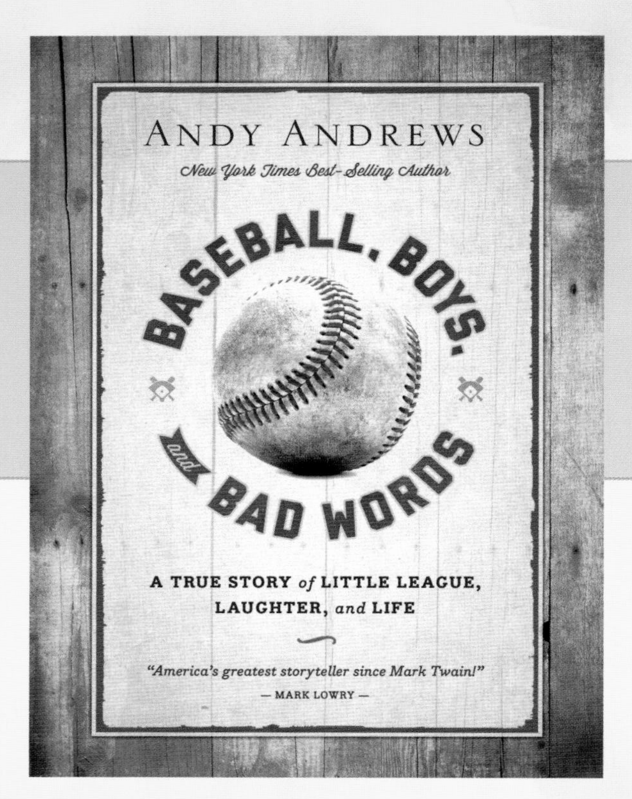

RECALL THE HILARITY AND MAGIC OF LITTLE LEAGUE BASEBALL.

Often called "the funniest tale ever told," this story will have you and your family laughing until you cry!

THOMAS NELSON
Since 1798

For more information, visit AndyAndrews.com.

9780529115768-A